Winnie-The-Pooh

By A.A.Milne
Originally published in 1926
Abridged and adapted by
Mars Starship Publishing
© 2022
Cover and illustrations: E.H.Shepard
www.MarsStarship.com

Winnie-The-Pooh
BOOK 2

CHAPTER VII

IN WHICH KANGA AND BABY ROO COME TO THE FOREST, AND PIGLET HAS A BATH

Nobody seemed to know where they came from, but there they were in the Forest: Kanga and Baby Roo. When Pooh asked Christopher Robin, "How did they come here?" Christopher Robin said, "In the Usual Way, if you know what I mean, Pooh," and Pooh, who didn't, said "Oh!" Then he nodded his head twice and said, "In the Usual Way. Ah!" Then he went to call upon his friend Piglet to see what *he* thought about it. And at Piglet's house he found Rabbit. So they all talked about it together.

"What I don't like about it is this," said Rabbit. "Here are we—you, Pooh, and you, Piglet, and Me—and suddenly——"

"And Eeyore," said Pooh.

"And Eeyore—and then suddenly——"

"And Owl," said Pooh.

"And Owl—and then all of a sudden——"

"Oh, and Eeyore," said Pooh. "I was forgetting *him*."

"Here—we—are," said Rabbit very slowly and carefully, "all—of—us, and then, suddenly, we wake up one morning and, what do we find? We find a Strange Animal among us. An animal of

5

whom we have never even heard before! An animal who carries her family about with her in her pocket! Suppose *I* carried *my* family about with me in *my* pocket, how many pockets should I want?"

"Sixteen," said Piglet.

"Seventeen, isn't it?" said Rabbit. "And one more for a handkerchief—that's eighteen. Eighteen pockets in one suit! I haven't time."

There was a long and thoughtful silence ... and then Pooh, who had been frowning very hard for some minutes, said: "*I* make it fifteen."

"What?" said Rabbit.

"Fifteen."

"Fifteen what?"

"Your family."

"What about them?"

Pooh rubbed his nose and said that he thought Rabbit had been talking about his family.

"Did I?" said Rabbit carelessly.

"Yes, you said——"

"Never mind, Pooh," said Piglet impatiently.

"The question is, What are we to do about Kanga?"

"Oh, I see," said Pooh.

"The best way," said Rabbit, "would be this. The best way would be to steal Baby Roo and hide him, and then when Kanga says, 'Where's Baby Roo?' we say, '*Aha!*'"

"*Aha!*" said Pooh, practising. "*Aha! Aha!* ... Of course," he went on, "we could say 'Aha!' even if we hadn't stolen Baby Roo."

"Pooh," said Rabbit kindly, "you haven't any brain."

"I know," said Pooh humbly.

"We say '*Aha!*' so that Kanga knows that *we* know where Baby Roo is. '*Aha!*' means 'We'll tell you where Baby Roo is, if you promise to go away from the Forest and never come back.' Now don't talk while I think."

Pooh went into a corner and tried saying 'Aha!' in that sort of voice. Sometimes it seemed to him that it did mean what Rabbit said, and sometimes it seemed to him that it didn't. "I suppose it's just practice," he thought. "I wonder if Kanga will have to practise too so as to understand it."

"There's just one thing," said Piglet, fidgeting a bit. "I was talking to Christopher Robin, and he said that a Kanga was Generally Regarded as One of the Fiercer Animals. I am not frightened of Fierce Animals in the ordinary way, but it is well known that, if One of the Fiercer Animals is Deprived of Its Young, it becomes as fierce as Two of the Fiercer Animals. In which case '*Aha!*' is perhaps a *foolish* thing to say."

"Piglet," said Rabbit, taking out a pencil, and licking the end of it, "you haven't any pluck."

"It is hard to be brave," said Piglet, sniffing slightly, "when you're only a Very Small Animal."

Rabbit, who had begun to write very busily, looked up and said:

"It is because you are a very small animal that you will be Useful in the adventure before us."

Piglet was so excited at the idea of being Useful, that he forgot to be frightened any more, and when Rabbit went on to say that Kangas were only Fierce during the winter months, being at other times of an Affectionate Disposition, he could hardly sit still, he was so eager to begin being useful at once.

"What about me?" said Pooh sadly. "I suppose *I* shan't be useful?"

"Never mind, Pooh," said Piglet comfortingly. "Another time perhaps."

"Without Pooh," said Rabbit solemnly as he sharpened his pencil, "the adventure would be impossible."

"Oh!" said Piglet, and tried not to look disappointed. But Pooh went into a corner of the room and said proudly to himself, "Impossible without Me! *That* sort of Bear."

"Now listen all of you," said Rabbit when he had finished writing, and Pooh and Piglet sat listening very eagerly with their mouths open. This was what Rabbit read out:

PLAN TO CAPTURE BABY ROO

1. *General Remarks.* Kanga runs faster than any of Us, even Me.
2. *More General Remarks.* Kanga never takes her eye off Baby Roo, except when he's safely buttoned up in her pocket
3. *Therefore.* If we are to capture Baby Roo, we must get a Long Start, because Kanga runs faster than any of Us, even Me. (*See* 1.)
4. *A Thought.* If Roo had jumped out of Kanga's pocket and Piglet had jumped in, Kanga wouldn't know the difference, because Piglet is a Very Small Animal.
5. Like Roo.
6. But Kanga would have to be looking the other way first, so as not to see Piglet jumping in.
7. See 2.
8. *Another Thought.* But if Pooh was talking to her very excitedly, she *might* look the other way for a moment.
9. And then I could run away with Roo.
10. Quickly.
11. And Kanga wouldn't discover the difference until Afterwards

Well, Rabbit read this out proudly, and for a little while after he had read it nobody said anything. And then Piglet, who had been opening and shutting his mouth without making any noise, managed to say very huskily:

"And—Afterwards?"

"How do you mean?"

"When Kanga *does* Discover the Difference?"

"Then we all say '*Aha!*'"

"All three of us?"

"Yes."

"Oh!"

"Why, what's the trouble, Piglet?"

"Nothing," said Piglet, "as long as *we all three* say it. As long as we all three say it," said Piglet, "I don't mind," he said, "but I shouldn't care to say '*Aha!*' by myself. It wouldn't sound *nearly* so well. By the way," he said, "you *are* quite sure about what you said about the winter months?"

"The winter months?"

"Yes, only being Fierce in the Winter Months."

"Oh, yes, yes, that's all right. Well, Pooh? You see what you have to do?"

"No," said Pooh Bear. "Not yet," he said. "What *do* I do?"

"Well, you just have to talk very hard to Kanga so as she doesn't notice anything."

"Oh! What about?"

"Anything you like."

"You mean like telling her a little bit of poetry or something?"

"That's it," said Rabbit. "Splendid. Now come along."

So they all went out to look for Kanga.

Kanga and Roo were spending a quiet afternoon in a sandy part of the Forest. Baby Roo was practising very small jumps in the sand, and falling down mouse-holes and climbing out of them, and Kanga was fidgeting about and saying "Just one more jump, dear, and then we must go home." And at that moment who should come stumping up the hill but Pooh.

"Good afternoon, Kanga."

"Good afternoon, Pooh."

"Look at me jumping," squeaked Roo, and fell into another mouse-hole.

"Hallo, Roo, my little fellow!"

"We were just going home," said Kanga. "Good afternoon, Rabbit. Good afternoon, Piglet."

Rabbit and Piglet, who had now come up from the other side of the hill, said "Good afternoon," and "Hallo, Roo," and Roo asked them to look at him jumping, so they stayed and looked.

And Kanga looked too....

"Oh, Kanga," said Pooh, after Rabbit had winked at him twice, "I don't know if you are interested in Poetry at all?"

"Hardly at all," said Kanga.

"Oh!" said Pooh.

"Roo, dear, just one more jump and then we must go home."

There was a short silence while Roo fell down another mouse-hole.

"Go on," said Rabbit in a loud whisper behind his paw.

"Talking of Poetry," said Pooh, "I made up a little piece as I was coming along. It went like this. Er—now let me see——"

"Fancy!" said Kanga. "Now Roo, dear——"

"You'll like this piece of poetry," said Rabbit.

"You'll love it," said Piglet.

"You must listen very carefully," said Rabbit.

"So as not to miss any of it," said Piglet.

"Oh, yes," said Kanga, but she still looked at Baby Roo.

"*How* did it go, Pooh?" said Rabbit.

Pooh gave a little cough and began.

LINES WRITTEN BY A BEAR OF VERY LITTLE BRAIN

On Monday, when the sun is hot

I wonder to myself a lot:

"Now is it true, or is it not,

"That what is which and which is what?"

On Tuesday, when it hails and snows,

The feeling on me grows and grows

That hardly anybody knows

If those are these or these are those.

On Wednesday, when the sky is blue,

And I have nothing else to do,

I sometimes wonder if it's true

That who is what and what is who.

On Thursday, when it starts to freeze

And hoar-frost twinkles on the trees,

How very readily one sees

That these are whose—but whose are these?

On Friday——

"Yes, it is, isn't it?" said Kanga, not waiting to hear what happened on Friday. "Just one more jump, Roo, dear, and then we really *must* be going."

Rabbit gave Pooh a hurrying-up sort of nudge.

"Talking of Poetry," said Pooh quickly, "have you ever noticed that tree right over there?"

"Where?" said Kanga. "Now, Roo——"

"Right over there," said Pooh, pointing behind Kanga's back.

"No," said Kanga. "Now jump in, Roo, dear, and we'll go home."

"You ought to look at that tree right over there," said Rabbit. "Shall I lift you in, Roo?" And he picked up Roo in his paws.

"I can see a bird in it from here," said Pooh. "Or is it a fish?"

"You ought to see that bird from here," said Rabbit. "Unless it's a fish."

"It isn't a fish, it's a bird," said Piglet.

"So it is," said Rabbit.

"Is it a starling or a blackbird?" said Pooh.

"That's the whole question," said Rabbit. "Is it a blackbird or a starling?"

And then at last Kanga did turn her head to look. And the moment that her head was turned, Rabbit said in a loud voice "In you go, Roo!" and in jumped Piglet into Kanga's pocket, and off scampered Rabbit, with Roo in his paws, as fast as he could.

"Why, where's Rabbit?" said Kanga, turning round again. "Are you all right, Roo, dear?"

Piglet made a squeaky Roo-noise from the bottom of Kanga's pocket.

"Rabbit had to go away," said Pooh. "I think he thought of something he had to go and see about suddenly."

"And Piglet?"

"I think Piglet thought of something at the same time. Suddenly."

"Well, we must be getting home," said Kanga. "Good-bye, Pooh." And in three large jumps she was gone.

Pooh looked after her as she went.

"I wish I could jump like that," he thought. "Some can and some can't. That's how it is."

But there were moments when Piglet wished that Kanga couldn't. Often, when he had had a long walk home through the Forest, he had wished that he were a bird; but now he thought jerkily to himself at the bottom of Kanga's pocket,"If this is really like flying, I   shall   never try it."

And as he went up in the air he said, "*Ooooooo!*" and as he came down he said, "*Ow!*" And he was saying,   "*Ooooooo-ow,   Ooooooo-ow, Ooooooo-ow*" all the way to Kanga's house.

Of course as soon as Kanga unbuttoned her pocket, she saw what had happened. Just for a moment, she thought she was frightened, and then she knew she wasn't; for she felt quite sure that Christopher Robin would never let any harm happen to Roo. So she said to herself, "If they are having a joke with me, I will have a joke with them."

"Now then, Roo, dear," she said, as she took Piglet out of her pocket. "Bed-time."

"*Aha!*" said Piglet, as well as he could after his Terrifying Journey. But it wasn't a very good "*Aha!*" and Kanga didn't seem to understand what it meant.

"Bath first," said Kanga in a cheerful voice.

"*Aha!*" said Piglet again, looking round anxiously for the others. But the others weren't there. Rabbit was playing with Baby Roo in his own house, and feeling more fond of him every minute, and Pooh, who had decided to be a Kanga, was still at the sandy place on the top of the Forest, practising jumps.

"I am not at all sure," said Kanga in a thoughtful voice, "that it wouldn't be a good idea to have a *cold* bath this evening. Would you like that, Roo, dear?"

Piglet, who had never been really fond of baths, shuddered a long indignant shudder, and said in as brave a voice as he could:

"Kanga, I see that the time has come to spleak painly."

"Funny little Roo," said Kanga, as she got the bath-water ready.

"I am *not* Roo," said Piglet loudly. "I am Piglet!"

"Yes, dear, yes," said Kanga soothingly. "And imitating Piglet's voice too! So clever of him," she went on, as she took a large bar of yellow soap out of the cupboard. "What *will* he be doing next?"

"Can't you *see*?" shouted Piglet. "Haven't you got *eyes*? *Look* at me!"

"I *am* looking, Roo, dear," said Kanga rather severely. "And you know what I told you yesterday about making faces. If you go on making faces like Piglet's, you will grow up to *look* like Piglet—and *then* think how sorry you will be. Now then, into the bath, and don't let me have to speak to you about it again."

Before he knew where he was, Piglet was in the bath, and Kanga was scrubbing him firmly with a large lathery flannel.

"Ow!" cried Piglet. "Let me out! I'm Piglet!"

"Don't open your mouth, dear, or the soap goes in," said Kanga. "There! What did I tell you?"

"You—you—you did it on purpose," spluttered Piglet, as soon as he could speak again ... and then accidentally had another mouthful of lathery flannel.

"That's right, dear, don't say anything," said Kanga, and in another minute Piglet was out of the bath, and being rubbed dry with a towel.

"Now," said Kanga, "there's your medicine, and then bed."

"W-w-what medicine?" said Piglet.

"To make you grow big and strong, dear. You don't want to grow up small and weak like Piglet, do you? Well, then!"

At that moment there was a knock at the door.

"Come in," said Kanga, and in came Christopher Robin.

"Christopher Robin, Christopher Robin!" cried Piglet. "Tell Kanga who I am! She keeps saying I'm Roo. I'm *not* Roo, am I?"

Christopher Robin looked at him very carefully, and shook his head.

"You can't be Roo," he said, "because I've just seen Roo playing in Rabbit's house."

"Well!" said Kanga. "Fancy that! Fancy my making a mistake like that."

"There you are!" said Piglet. "I told you so. I'm Piglet."

Christopher Robin shook his head again.

"Oh, you're not Piglet," he said. "I know Piglet well, and he's *quite* a different colour."

Piglet began to say that this was because he had just had a bath, and then he thought that perhaps he wouldn't say that, and as he opened his mouth to say something else, Kanga slipped the medicine spoon in, and then patted him on the back and told him that it was really quite a nice taste when you got used to it.

"I knew it wasn't Piglet," said Kanga. "I wonder who it can be."

"Perhaps it's some relation of Pooh's," said Christopher Robin. "What about a nephew or an uncle or something?"

Kanga agreed that this was probably what it was, and said that they would have to call it by some name.

"I shall call it Pootel," said Christopher Robin. "Henry Pootel for short."

And just when it was decided, Henry Pootel wriggled out of Kanga's arms and jumped to the ground. To his great joy Christopher Robin had left the door open. Never had Henry Pootel Piglet run so fast as he ran then, and he didn't stop running until he had got quite close to his house. But when he was a hundred yards away he stopped running, and rolled the rest of the way home, so as to get his own nice comfortable colour again....

So Kanga and Roo stayed in the Forest. And every Tuesday Roo spent the day with his great friend Rabbit, and every Tuesday Kanga spent the day with her great friend Pooh, teaching him to jump, and every Tuesday Piglet spent the day with his great friend Christopher Robin. So they were all happy again.

CHAPTER VIII

IN WHICH CHRISTOPHER ROBIN LEADS AN EXPOTITION TO THE NORTH POLE

One fine day Pooh had stumped up to the top of the Forest to see if his friend Christopher Robin was interested in Bears at all. At breakfast that morning (a simple meal of marmalade spread lightly over a honeycomb or two) he had suddenly thought of a new song. It began like this:

"Sing Ho! for the life of a Bear."

When he had got as far as this, he scratched his head, and thought to himself "That's a very good start for a song, but what about the second line?" He tried singing "Ho," two or three times, but it didn't seem to help. "Perhaps it would be better," he thought, "if I sang Hi for the life of a Bear." So he sang it ... but it wasn't. "Very well, then," he said, "I shall sing that first line twice, and perhaps if I sing it very quickly, I shall find myself singing the third and fourth lines before I have time to think of them, and that will be a Good Song. Now then:"

Sing Ho! for the life of a Bear!

Sing Ho! for the life of a Bear!

I don't much mind if it rains or snows,

'Cos I've got a lot of honey on my nice new nose,

I don't much care if it snows or thaws,

'Cos I've got a lot of honey on my nice clean paws!

Sing Ho! for a Bear!

Sing Ho! for a Pooh!

And I'll have a little something in an hour or two!

He was so pleased with this song that he sang it all the way to the top of the Forest, "and if I go on singing it much longer," he thought, "it will be time for the little something, and then the last line won't be true." So he turned it into a hum instead.

Christopher Robin was sitting outside his door, putting on his Big Boots. As soon as he saw the Big Boots, Pooh knew that an Adventure was going to happen, and he brushed the honey off his nose with the back of his paw, and spruced himself up as well as he could, so as to look Ready for Anything.

"Good-morning, Christopher Robin," he called out.

"Hallo, Pooh Bear. I can't get this boot on."

"That's bad," said Pooh.

"Do you think you could very kindly lean against me, 'cos I keep pulling so hard that I fall over backwards."

Pooh sat down, dug his feet into the ground, and pushed hard against Christopher Robin's back, and Christopher Robin pushed hard against his, and pulled and pulled at his boot until he had got it on.

"And that's that," said Pooh. "What do we do next?"

"We are all going on an Expedition," said Christopher Robin, as he got up and brushed himself. "Thank you, Pooh."

"Going on an Expotition?" said Pooh eagerly. "I don't think I've ever been on one of those. Where are we going to on this Expotition?"

"Expedition, silly old Bear. It's got an 'x' in it."

"Oh!" said Pooh. "I know." But he didn't really.

"We're going to discover the North Pole."

"Oh!" said Pooh again. "What *is* the North Pole?" he asked.

"It's just a thing you discover," said Christopher Robin carelessly, not being quite sure himself.

"Oh! I see," said Pooh. "Are bears any good at discovering it?"

"Of course they are. And Rabbit and Kanga and all of you. It's an Expedition. That's what an Expedition means. A long line of everybody. You'd better tell the others to get ready, while I see if my gun's all right. And we must all bring Provisions."

"Bring what?"

"Things to eat."

"Oh!" said Pooh happily. "I thought you said Provisions. I'll go and tell them." And he stumped off.

The first person he met was Rabbit.

"Hallo, Rabbit," he said, "is that you?"

"Let's pretend it isn't," said Rabbit, "and see what happens."

"I've got a message for you."

"I'll give it to him."

"We're all going on an Expotition with Christopher Robin!"

"What is it when we're on it?"

"A sort of boat, I think," said Pooh.

"Oh! that sort."

"Yes. And we're going to discover a Pole or something. Or was it a Mole? Anyhow we're going to discover it."

"We are, are we?" said Rabbit.

"Yes. And we've got to bring Pro—things to eat with us. In case we want to eat them. Now I'm going down to Piglet's. Tell Kanga, will you?"

He left Rabbit and hurried down to Piglet's house. The Piglet was sitting on the ground at the door of his house blowing happily at a dandelion, and wondering whether it would be this year, next year, sometime or never. He had just discovered that it would be never, and was trying to remember what "*it*" was, and hoping it wasn't anything nice, when Pooh came up.

"Oh! Piglet," said Pooh excitedly, "we're going on an Expotition, all of us, with things to eat. To discover something."

"To discover what?" said Piglet anxiously.

"Oh! just something."

"Nothing fierce?"

"Christopher Robin didn't say anything about fierce. He just said it had an 'x'."

"It isn't their necks I mind," said Piglet earnestly. "It's their teeth. But if Christopher Robin is coming I don't mind anything."

In a little while they were all ready at the top of the Forest, and the Expotition started. First came Christopher Robin and Rabbit, then Piglet and Pooh; then Kanga, with Roo in her pocket, and

33

Owl; then Eeyore; and, at the end, in a long line, all Rabbit's friends-and-relations.

"I didn't ask them," explained Rabbit carelessly. "They just came. They always do. They can march at the end, after Eeyore."

"What I say," said Eeyore, "is that it's unsettling. I didn't want to come on this Expo—what Pooh said. I only came to oblige. But here I am; and if I am the end of the Expo—what we're talking about—then let me *be* the end. But if, every time I want to sit down for a little rest, I have to brush away half a dozen of Rabbit's smaller friends-and-relations first, then this isn't an Expo—whatever it is—at all, it's simply a Confused Noise. That's what *I* say."

"I see what Eeyore means," said Owl. "If you ask me——"

"I'm not asking anybody," said Eeyore. "I'm just telling everybody. We can look for the North Pole, or we can play 'Here we go gathering Nuts and May' with the end part of an ant's nest. It's all the same to me."

There was a shout from the top of the line.

"Come on!" called Christopher Robin.

"Come on!" called Pooh and Piglet

"Come on!" called Owl.

"We're starting," said Rabbit. "I must go." And he hurried off to the front of the Expotition with Christopher Robin.

"All right," said Eeyore. "We're going. Only Don't Blame Me."

So off they all went to discover the Pole. And as they walked, they chattered to each other of this and that, all except Pooh, who was making up a song.

"This is the first verse," he said to Piglet, when he was ready with it.

"First verse of what?"

"My song."

"What song?"

"This one."

"Which one?"

"Well, if you listen, Piglet, you'll hear it."

"How do you know I'm not listening?"

Pooh couldn't answer that one, so he began to sing.

They all went off to discover the Pole,

    Owl and Piglet and Rabbit and all;

It's a Thing you Discover, as I've been tole

    By Owl and Piglet and Rabbit and all.

Eeyore, Christopher Robin and Pooh

And Rabbit's relations all went too—

And where the Pole was none of them knew....

Sing Hey! for Owl and Rabbit and all!

"Hush!" said Christopher Robin turning round to Pooh, "we're just coming to a Dangerous Place."

"Hush!" said Pooh turning round quickly to Piglet.

"Hush!" said Piglet to Kanga.

"Hush!" said Kanga to Owl, while Roo said "Hush!" several times to himself very quietly.

"Hush!" said Owl to Eeyore.

"*Hush!*" said Eeyore in a terrible voice to all Rabbit's friends-and-relations, and "Hush!" they said hastily to each other all down the line, until it got to the last one of all. And the last and smallest friend-and-relation was so upset to find that the whole Expotition was saying "Hush!" to *him*, that he buried himself head downwards in a crack in the ground, and stayed there for two days until the danger was over, and then went home in a great hurry, and lived quietly with his Aunt ever-afterwards. His name was Alexander Beetle.

They had come to a stream which twisted and tumbled between high rocky banks, and Christopher Robin saw at once how dangerous it was.

"It's just the place," he explained, "for an Ambush."

"What sort of bush?" whispered Pooh to Piglet. "A gorse-bush?"

"My dear Pooh," said Owl in his superior way, "don't you know what an Ambush is?"

"Owl," said Piglet, looking round at him severely, "Pooh's whisper was a perfectly private whisper, and there was no need——"

"An Ambush," said Owl, "is a sort of Surprise."

"So is a gorse-bush sometimes," said Pooh.

"An Ambush, as I was about to explain to Pooh," said Piglet, "is a sort of Surprise."

"If people jump out at you suddenly, that's an Ambush," said Owl.

"It's an Ambush, Pooh, when people jump at you suddenly," explained Piglet.

Pooh, who now knew what an Ambush was, said that a gorse-bush had sprung at him suddenly one day when he fell off a tree, and he had taken six days to get all the prickles out of himself.

"We are not *talking* about gorse-bushes," said Owl a little crossly.

"I am," said Pooh.

They were climbing very cautiously up the stream now, going from rock to rock, and after they had gone a little way they came to a place where the banks widened out at each side, so that on each side of the water there was a level strip of grass on which they could sit down and rest. As soon as he saw this, Christopher Robin called "Halt!" and they all sat down and rested.

"I think," said Christopher Robin, "that we ought to eat all our Provisions now, so that we shan't have so much to carry."

"Eat all our what?" said Pooh.

"All that we've brought," said Piglet, getting to work.

"That's a good idea," said Pooh, and he got to work too.

"Have you all got something?" asked Christopher Robin with his mouth full.

"All except me," said Eeyore. "As Usual." He looked round at them in his melancholy way. "I suppose none of you are sitting on a thistle by any chance?"

"I believe I am," said Pooh. "Ow!" He got up, and looked behind him. "Yes, I was. I thought so."

"Thank you, Pooh. If you've quite finished with it." He moved across to Pooh's place, and began to eat.

"It don't do them any Good, you know, sitting on them," he went on, as he looked up munching. "Takes all the Life out of them. Remember that another time, all of you. A little Consideration, a little Thought for Others, makes all the difference."

As soon as he had finished his lunch Christopher Robin whispered to Rabbit, and Rabbit said "Yes, yes, of course," and they walked a little way up the stream together.

"I didn't want the others to hear," said Christopher Robin.

"Quite so," said Rabbit, looking important.

"It's—I wondered—It's only—Rabbit, I suppose *you* don't know, What does the North Pole *look* like?"

"Well," said Rabbit, stroking his whiskers. "Now you're asking me."

"I did know once, only I've sort of forgotten," said Christopher Robin carelessly.

"It's a funny thing," said Rabbit, "but I've sort of forgotten too, although I did know *once*."

"I suppose it's just a pole stuck in the ground?"

"Sure to be a pole," said Rabbit, "because of calling it a pole, and if it's a pole, well, I should think it would be sticking in the ground, shouldn't you, because there'd be nowhere else to stick it."

"Yes, that's what I thought."

"The only thing," said Rabbit, "is, *where is it sticking*?"

"That's what we're looking for," said Christopher Robin.

They went back to the others. Piglet was lying on his back, sleeping peacefully. Roo was washing his face and paws in the stream, while Kanga explained to everybody proudly that this was the first time he had ever washed his face himself, and Owl was telling Kanga an Interesting Anecdote full of long words like Encyclopædia and Rhododendron to which Kanga wasn't listening.

"I don't hold with all this washing," grumbled Eeyore. "This modern Behind-the-ears nonsense. What do *you* think, Pooh?"

"Well," said Pooh, "*I* think——"

But we shall never know what Pooh thought, for there came a sudden squeak from Roo, a splash, and a loud cry of alarm from Kanga.

"So much for *washing*," said Eeyore.

"Roo's fallen in!" cried Rabbit, and he and Christopher Robin came rushing down to the rescue.

"Look at me swimming!" squeaked Roo from the middle of his pool, and was hurried down a waterfall into the next pool.

"Are you all right, Roo dear?" called Kanga anxiously.

"Yes!" said Roo. "Look at me sw——" and down he went over the next waterfall into another pool.

Everybody was doing something to help. Piglet, wide awake suddenly, was jumping up and down and making "Oo, I say" noises; Owl was explaining that in a case of Sudden and Temporary Immersion the Important Thing was to keep the Head Above Water; Kanga was jumping along the bank, saying "Are you *sure* you're all right, Roo dear?" to which Roo, from whatever pool he was in at the moment, was answering "Look at me swimming!" Eeyore had turned round and hung his tail over the first pool into which Roo fell, and with his back to the accident was grumbling quietly to himself, and saying, "All this washing; but catch on to my tail, little Roo, and you'll be all right"; and, Christopher Robin and Rabbit came hurrying past Eeyore, and were calling out to the others in front of them.

"All right, Roo, I'm coming," called Christopher Robin.

"Get something across the stream lower down, some of you fellows," called Rabbit.

But Pooh was getting something. Two pools below Roo he was standing with a long pole in his paws, and Kanga came up and took one end of it, and between them they held it across the lower part of the pool; and Roo, still bubbling proudly, "Look at me swimming," drifted up against it, and climbed out.

"Did you see me swimming?" squeaked Roo excitedly, while Kanga scolded him and rubbed him down. "Pooh, did you see me swimming? That's called swimming, what I was doing. Rabbit, did you see what I was doing? Swimming. Hallo, Piglet! I say, Piglet! What do you think I was doing! Swimming! Christopher Robin, did you see me——"

But Christopher Robin wasn't listening. He was looking at Pooh.

"Pooh," he said, "where did you find that pole?"

Pooh looked at the pole in his hands.

"I just found it," he said. "I thought it ought to be useful. I just picked it up."

"Pooh," said Christopher Robin solemnly, "the Expedition is over. You have found the North Pole!"

"Oh!" said Pooh.

Eeyore was sitting with his tail in the water when they all got back to him.

"Tell Roo to be quick, somebody," he said. "My tail's getting cold. I don't want to mention it, but I just mention it. I don't want to complain but there it is. My tail's cold."

"Here I am!" squeaked Roo.

"Oh, there you are."

"Did you see me swimming?"

Eeyore took his tail out of the water, and swished it from side to side.

"As I expected," he said. "Lost all feeling. Numbed it. That's what it's done. Numbed it. Well, as long as nobody minds, I suppose it's all right."

"Poor old Eeyore. I'll dry it for you," said Christopher Robin, and he took out his handkerchief and rubbed it up.

"Thank you, Christopher Robin. You're the only one who seems to understand about tails. They don't think—that's what the matter with some of these others. They've no imagination. A tail isn't a tail to *them*, it's just a Little Bit Extra at the back."

"Never mind, Eeyore," said Christopher Robin, rubbing his hardest. "Is *that* better?"

"It's feeling more like a tail perhaps. It Belongs again, if you know what I mean."

"Hullo, Eeyore," said Pooh, coming up to them with his pole.

"Hullo, Pooh. Thank you for asking, but I shall be able to use it again in a day or two."

"Use what?" said Pooh.

"What we are talking about."

"I wasn't talking about anything," said Pooh, looking puzzled.

"My mistake again. I thought you were saying how sorry you were about my tail, being all numb, and could you do anything to help?"

"No," said Pooh. "That wasn't me," he said. He thought for a little and then suggested helpfully, "Perhaps it was somebody else."

"Well, thank him for me when you see him."

Pooh looked anxiously at Christopher Robin.

"Pooh's found the North Pole," said Christopher Robin. "Isn't that lovely?"

Pooh looked modestly down.

"Is that it?" said Eeyore.

"Yes," said Christopher Robin.

"Is that what we were looking for?"

"Yes," said Pooh.

"Oh!" said Eeyore. "Well, anyhow—it didn't rain," he said.

They stuck the pole in the ground, and Christopher Robin tied a message on to it.

NORTH POLE

DISCOVERED BY POOH

POOH FOUND IT.

Then they all went home again. And I think, but I am not quite sure, that Roo had a hot bath and went straight to bed. But Pooh went back to his own house, and feeling very proud of what he had done, had a little something to revive himself.

CHAPTER IX

IN WHICH PIGLET IS ENTIRELY SURROUNDED BY WATER

It rained and it rained and it rained. Piglet told himself that never in all his life, and *he* was goodness knows *how* old—three, was it, or four?—never had he seen so much rain. Days and days and days.

"If only," he thought, as he looked out of the window, "I had been in Pooh's house, or Christopher Robin's house, or Rabbit's house when it began to rain, then I should have had Company all this time, instead of being here all alone, with nothing to do except wonder when it will stop." And he imagined himself with Pooh, saying, "Did you ever see such rain, Pooh?" and Pooh saying, "Isn't it *awful*, Piglet?" and Piglet saying, "I wonder how it is over Christopher Robin's way" and Pooh saying, "I should think poor old Rabbit is about flooded out by this time." It would have been jolly to talk like this, and really, it wasn't much good having anything exciting like floods, if you couldn't share them with somebody.

For it was rather exciting. The little dry ditches in which Piglet had nosed about so often had become streams, the little streams across which he had splashed were rivers, and the river, between whose steep banks they had played so happily, had sprawled out of its own bed and was taking up so much room everywhere, that Piglet was beginning to wonder whether it would be coming into *his* bed soon.

"It's a little Anxious," he said to himself, "to be a Very Small Animal Entirely Surrounded by Water. Christopher Robin and Pooh could escape by Climbing Trees, and Kanga could escape by Jumping, and Rabbit could escape by Burrowing, and Owl could escape by Flying, and Eeyore could escape by—by Making a Loud Noise Until Rescued, and here am I, surrounded by water and I can't do *anything*."

It went on raining, and every day the water got a little higher, until now it was nearly up to Piglet's window ... and still he hadn't done anything.

"There's Pooh," he thought to himself. "Pooh hasn't much Brain, but he never comes to any harm. He does silly things and they turn out right. There's Owl. Owl hasn't exactly got Brain, but he Knows Things. He would know the Right Thing to Do when Surrounded by Water. There's Rabbit.

He hasn't Learnt in Books, but he can always Think of a Clever Plan. There's Kanga. She isn't Clever, Kanga isn't, but she would be so anxious about Roo that she would do a Good Thing to Do without thinking about It. And then there's Eeyore. And Eeyore is so miserable anyhow that he wouldn't mind about this. But I wonder what Christopher Robin would do?"

Then suddenly he remembered a story which Christopher Robin had told him about a man on a desert island who had written something in a bottle and thrown it in the sea; and Piglet thought that if he wrote something in a bottle and threw it in the water, perhaps somebody would come and rescue *him*!

He left the window and began to search his house, all of it that wasn't under water, and at last he found a pencil and a small piece of dry paper, and a bottle with a cork to it. And he wrote on one side of the paper:

HELP!

PIGLET (ME)

and on the other side:

IT'S ME PIGLET, HELP HELP.

Then he put the paper in the bottle, and he corked the bottle up as tightly as he could, and he leant out of his window as far as he could lean without falling in, and he threw the bottle as far as he could throw—*splash!*—and in a little while it bobbed up again on the water; and he watched it floating slowly away in the distance, until his eyes ached with looking, and sometimes he thought it was the bottle, and sometimes he thought it was just a ripple on the water which he was following, and then suddenly he knew that he would never see it again and that he had done all that he could do to save himself.

"So now," he thought, "somebody else will have to do something, and I hope they will do it soon, because if they don't I shall have to swim, which I can't, so I hope they do it soon." And then he gave a very long sigh and said, "I wish Pooh were here. It's so much more friendly with two."

When the rain began Pooh was asleep. It rained, and it rained, and it rained, and he slept and he slept and he slept. He had had a tiring day. You remember how he discovered the North Pole; well, he was so proud of this that he asked Christopher Robin if there were any other Poles such as a Bear of Little Brain might discover.

"There's a South Pole," said Christopher Robin, "and I expect there's an East Pole and a West Pole, though people don't like talking about them."

Pooh was very excited when he heard this, and suggested that they should have an Expotition to discover the East Pole, but Christopher Robin had thought of something else to do with Kanga; so Pooh went out to discover the East Pole by himself. Whether he discovered it or not, I forget; but he was so tired when he got home that, in the very middle of his supper, after he had been eating for little more than half-an-hour, he fell fast asleep in his chair, and slept and slept and slept.

Then suddenly he was dreaming. He was at the East Pole, and it was a very cold pole with the coldest sort of snow and ice all over it. He had found a bee-hive to sleep in, but there wasn't room for his legs, so he had left them outside. And Wild Woozles, such as inhabit the East Pole, came and nibbled all the fur off his legs to make nests for their Young. And the more they nibbled, the colder his legs got, until suddenly he woke up with an *Ow!*—and there he was, sitting in his chair with his feet in the water, and water all round him!

He splashed to his door and looked out.. .

"This is Serious," said Pooh. "I must have an Escape."

So he took his largest pot of honey and escaped with it to a broad branch of his tree, well above the water, and then he climbed down again and escaped with another pot ... and when the whole Escape was finished, there was Pooh sitting on his branch, dangling his legs, and there, beside him, were ten pots of honey....

Two days later, there was Pooh, sitting on his branch, dangling his legs, and there, beside him, were four pots of honey....

Three days later, there was Pooh, sitting on his branch, dangling his legs, and there beside him, was one pot of honey.

Four days later, there was Pooh ...

And it was on the morning of the fourth day that Piglet's bottle came floating past him, and with one loud cry of "Honey!" Pooh plunged into the water, seized the bottle, and struggled back to his tree again.

"Bother!" said Pooh, as he opened it. "All that wet for nothing. What's that bit of paper doing?"

He took it out and looked at it.

"It's a Missage," he said to himself, "that's what it is. And that letter is a 'P,' and so is that, and so is that, and 'P' means 'Pooh,' so it's a very important Missage to me, and I can't read it. I must find Christopher Robin or Owl or Piglet, one of those Clever Readers who can read things, and they will tell me what this missage means. Only I can't swim. Bother!"

Then he had an idea, and I think that for a Bear of Very Little Brain, it was a good idea. He said to himself:

"If a bottle can float, then a jar can float, and if a jar floats, I can sit on the top of it, if it's a very big jar."

So he took his biggest jar, and corked it up. "All boats have to have a name," he said, "so I shall call mine *The Floating Bear*." And with these words he dropped his boat into the water and jumped in after it.

For a little while Pooh and *The Floating Bear* were uncertain as to which of them was meant to be on the top, but after trying one or two different positions, they settled down with *The Floating Bear* underneath and Pooh triumphantly astride it, paddling vigorously with his feet.

Christopher Robin lived at the very top of the Forest. It rained, and it rained, and it rained, but the water couldn't come up to *his* house. It was rather jolly to look down into the valleys and see the water all round him, but it rained so hard that he stayed indoors most of the time, and thought about things. Every morning he went out with his umbrella and put a stick in the place where the water came up to, and every next morning he went out and couldn't see his stick any more, so he put another stick in the place where the water came up to, and then he walked home again, and each morning he had a shorter way to walk than he had had the morning before. On the morning of the fifth day he saw the water all round him, and knew that for the first time in his life he was on a real island. Which was very exciting.

It was on this morning that Owl came flying over the water to say "How do you do," to his friend Christopher Robin.

"I say, Owl," said Christopher Robin, "isn't this fun? I'm on an island!"

"The atmospheric conditions have been very unfavourable lately," said Owl.

"The what?"

"It has been raining," explained Owl.

"Yes," said Christopher Robin. "It has."

"The flood-level has reached an unprecedented height."

"The who?"

"There's a lot of water about," explained Owl.

"Yes," said Christopher Robin, "there is."

"However, the prospects are rapidly becoming more favourable. At any moment——"

"Have you seen Pooh?"

"No. At any moment——"

"I hope he's all right," said Christopher Robin. "I've been wondering about him. I expect Piglet's with him. Do you think they're all right, Owl?"

"I expect so. You see, at any moment——"

"Do go and see, Owl. Because Pooh hasn't got very much brain, and he might do something silly, and I do love him so, Owl. Do you see, Owl?"

"That's all right," said Owl. "I'll go. Back directly." And he flew off.

In a little while he was back again.

"Pooh isn't there," he said.

"Not there?"

"Has *been* there. He's been sitting on a branch of his tree outside his house with nine pots of honey. But he isn't there now."

"Oh, Pooh!" cried Christopher Robin. "Where *are* you?"

"Here I am," said a growly voice behind him.

"Pooh!"

They rushed into each other's arms.

"How did you get here, Pooh?" asked Christopher Robin, when he was ready to talk again.

"On my boat," said Pooh proudly. "I had a Very Important Missage sent me in a bottle, and owing to having got some water in my eyes, I couldn't read it, so I brought it to you. On my boat."

With these proud words he gave Christopher Robin the missage.

"But it's from Piglet!" cried Christopher Robin when he had read it.

"Isn't there anything about Pooh in it?" asked Bear, looking over his shoulder.

Christopher Robin read the message aloud.

"Oh, are those 'P's' piglets? I thought they were poohs."

"We must rescue him at once! I thought he was with *you*, Pooh. Owl, could you rescue him on your back?"

"I don't think so," said Owl, after grave thought. "It is doubtful if the necessary dorsal muscles——"

"Then would you fly to him at *once* and say that Rescue is Coming? And Pooh and I will think of a Rescue and come as quick as ever we can. Oh, don't *talk*, Owl, go on quick!" And, still thinking of something to say, Owl flew off.

"Now then, Pooh," said Christopher Robin, "where's your boat?"

"I ought to say," explained Pooh as they walked down to the shore of the island, "that it isn't just an ordinary sort of boat. Sometimes it's a Boat, and sometimes it's more of an Accident. It all depends."

"Depends on what?"

"On whether I'm on the top of it or underneath it."

"Oh! Well, where is it?"

"There!" said Pooh, pointing proudly to *The Floating Bear*.

It wasn't what Christopher Robin expected, and the more he looked at it, the more he thought what a Brave and Clever Bear Pooh was, and the more Christopher Robin thought this, the more Pooh looked modestly down his nose and tried to pretend he wasn't.

"But it's too small for two of us," said Christopher Robin sadly.

"Three of us with Piglet."

"That makes it smaller still. Oh, Pooh Bear, what shall we do?"

And then this Bear, Pooh Bear, Winnie-the-Pooh, F.O.P. (Friend of Piglet's), R.C. (Rabbit's Companion), P.D. (Pole Discoverer), E.C. and T.F. (Eeyore's Comforter and Tail-finder)—in fact, Pooh himself—said something so clever that Christopher Robin could only look at him with mouth open and eyes staring, wondering if this was really the Bear of Very Little Brain whom he had known and loved so long.

"We might go in your umbrella," said Pooh.

"?"

"We might go in your umbrella," said Pooh.

"? ?"

"We might go in your umbrella," said Pooh.

"!!!!!!"

For suddenly Christopher Robin saw that they might. He opened his umbrella and put it point downwards in the water. It floated but wobbled. Pooh got in. He was just beginning to say that it was all right now, when he found that it wasn't, so after a short drink which he didn't really want he waded back to Christopher Robin. Then they both got in together, and it wobbled no longer.

"I shall call this boat *The Brain of Pooh*," said Christopher Robin, and *The Brain of Pooh* set sail forthwith in a south-westerly direction, revolving gracefully.

You can imagine Piglet's joy when at last the ship came in sight of him. In after-years he liked to think that he had been in Very Great Danger during the Terrible Flood, but the only danger he had really been in was in the last half-hour of his imprisonment, when Owl, who had just flown up, sat on a branch of his tree to comfort him, and told him a very long story about an aunt who had once laid a seagull's egg by mistake, and the story went on and on, rather like this sentence, until Piglet who was listening out of his window without much hope, went to sleep quietly and naturally, slipping slowly out of the window towards the water until he was only hanging on by his toes, at which moment luckily, a sudden loud squawk from Owl, which was really part of the story, being what his aunt said, woke the Piglet up and just gave him time to jerk himself back into safety and say, "How interesting, and did she?" when—well, you can imagine his joy when at last he saw the good ship, *Brain of Pooh* (*Captain*, C. Robin; *1st Mate*, P. Bear) coming over the sea to rescue him. Christopher Robin and Pooh again....

And that is really the end of the story, and I am very tired after that last sentence, I think I shall stop there.

CHAPTER X

IN WHICH CHRISTOPHER ROBIN GIVES POOH A PARTY, AND WE SAY GOOD-BYE

One day when the sun had come back over the Forest, bringing with it the scent of may, and all the streams of the Forest were tinkling happily to find themselves their own pretty shape again, and the little pools lay dreaming of the life they had seen and the big things they had done, and in the warmth and quiet of the Forest the cuckoo was trying over his voice carefully and listening to see if he liked it, and wood-pigeons were complaining gently to themselves in their lazy comfortable way that it was the other fellow's fault, but it didn't matter very much; on such a day as this Christopher Robin whistled in a special way he had, and Owl came flying out of the Hundred Acre Wood to see what was wanted.

"Owl," said Christopher Robin, "I am going to give a party."

"You are, are you?" said Owl.

"And it's to be a special sort of party, because it's because of what Pooh did when he did what he did to save Piglet from the flood."

"Oh, that's what it's for, is it?" said Owl.

"Yes, so will you tell Pooh as quickly as you can, and all the others, because it will be to-morrow."

"Oh, it will, will it?" said Owl, still being as helpful as possible.

"So will you go and tell them, Owl?"

Owl tried to think of something very wise to say, but couldn't, so he flew off to tell the others. And the first person he told was Pooh.

"Pooh," he said, "Christopher Robin is giving a party."

"Oh!" said Pooh. And then seeing that Owl expected him to say something else, he said "Will there be those little cake things with pink sugar icing?"

Owl felt that it was rather beneath him to talk about little cake things with pink sugar icing, so he told Pooh exactly what Christopher Robin had said, and flew off to Eeyore.

"A party for Me?" thought Pooh to himself. "How grand!" And he began to wonder if all the other animals would know that it was a special Pooh Party, and if Christopher Robin had told them about *The Floating Bear* and the *Brain of Pooh* and all the wonderful ships he had invented and sailed on, and he began to think how awful it would be if everybody had forgotten about it, and nobody quite knew what the party was for; and the more he thought like this, the more the party got muddled in his mind, like a dream when nothing goes right. And the dream began to sing itself over in his head until it became a sort of song. It was an

ANXIOUS POOH SONG.

3 Cheers for Pooh!

(*For Who?*)

For Pooh—

(*Why what did he do?*)

I thought you knew;

He saved his friend from a wetting!

3 Cheers for Bear!

(*For where?*)

For Bear—

He couldn't swim,

But he rescued him!

(*He rescued who?*)

Oh, listen, do!

I am talking of Pooh—

(*Of who?*)

Of Pooh!

(*I'm sorry I keep forgetting*).

Well, Pooh was a Bear of Enormous Brain

(*Just say it again!*)

Of enormous brain—

(*Of enormous what?*)

Well, he ate a lot,

And I don't know if he could swim or not,

But he managed to float

On a sort of boat

(*On a sort of what?*)

Well, a sort of pot—

So now let's give him three hearty cheers

(*So now let's give him three hearty whiches?*)

And hope he'll be with us for years and years,

And grow in health and wisdom and riches!

3 Cheers for Pooh!

(*For who?*)

For Pooh—

3 Cheers for Bear!

(*For where?*)

For Bear—

3 Cheers for the wonderful Winnie-the-Pooh!

(*Just tell me, somebody*—WHAT DID HE DO?)

While this was going on inside him, Owl was talking to Eeyore.

"Eeyore," said Owl, "Christopher Robin is giving a party."

"Very interesting," said Eeyore. "I suppose they will be sending me down the odd bits which got trodden on. Kind and Thoughtful. Not at all, don't mention it."

"There is an Invitation for you."

"What's that like?"

"An Invitation!"

"Yes, I heard you. Who dropped it?"

"This isn't anything to eat, it's asking you to the party. To-morrow."

Eeyore shook his head slowly.

"You mean Piglet. The little fellow with the excited ears. That's Piglet. I'll tell him."

"No, no!" said Owl, getting quite fussy. "It's you!"

"Are you sure?"

"Of course I'm sure. Christopher Robin said 'All of them! Tell all of them.'"

"All of them, except Eeyore?"

"All of them," said Owl sulkily.

"Ah!" said Eeyore. "A mistake, no doubt, but still, I shall come. Only don't blame *me* if it rains."

But it didn't rain. Christopher Robin had made a long table out of some long pieces of wood, and they all sat round it. Christopher Robin sat at one end, and Pooh sat at the other, and between them on one side were Owl and Eeyore and Piglet, and between them on the other side were Rabbit, and Roo and Kanga. And all Rabbit's friends and relations spread themselves about on the grass, and waited hopefully in case anybody spoke to them, or dropped anything, or asked them the time.

It was the first party to which Roo had ever been, and he was very excited. As soon as ever they had sat down he began to talk.

"Hallo, Pooh!" he squeaked.

"Hallo, Roo!" said Pooh.

Roo jumped up and down in his seat for a little while and then began again.

"Hallo, Piglet!" he squeaked.

Piglet waved a paw at him, being too busy to say anything.

"Hallo, Eeyore!" said Roo.

Eeyore nodded gloomily at him. "It will rain soon, you see if it doesn't," he said.

Roo looked to see if it didn't, and it didn't, so he said "Hallo, Owl!"—and Owl said "Hallo, my little fellow," in a kindly way, and went on telling Christopher Robin about an accident which had nearly happened to a friend of his whom

Christopher Robin didn't know, and Kanga said to Roo, "Drink up your milk first, dear, and talk afterwards." So Roo, who was drinking his milk, tried to say that he could do both at once ... and had to be patted on the back and dried for quite a long time afterwards.

When they had all nearly eaten enough, Christopher Robin banged on the table with his spoon, and everybody stopped talking and was very silent, except Roo who was just finishing a loud attack of hiccups and trying to look as if it was one of Rabbit's relations.

"This party," said Christopher Robin, "is a party because of what someone did, and we all know who it was, and it's his party, because of what he did, and I've got a present for him and here it is." Then he felt about a little and whispered, "Where is it?"

While he was looking, Eeyore coughed in an impressive way and began to speak.

"Friends," he said, "including oddments, it is a great pleasure, or perhaps I had better say it has been a pleasure so far, to see you at my party. What I did was nothing. Any of you—except Rabbit and Owl and Kanga—would have done the same. Oh, and Pooh. My remarks do not, of course, apply to Piglet and Roo, because they are too small. Any of you would have done the same. But it just happened to be Me. It was not, I need hardly say, with an idea of getting what Christopher Robin is looking for now"—and he put his front leg to his mouth and said in a loud whisper, "Try under the table"—"that I did what I did—but because I feel that we should all do what we can to help. I feel that we should all——"

"H—hup!" said Roo accidentally.

"Roo, dear!" said Kanga reproachfully.

"Was it me?" asked Roo, a little surprised.

"What's Eeyore talking about?" Piglet whispered to Pooh.

"I don't know," said Pooh rather dolefully.

"I thought this was *your* party."

"I thought it was *once*. But I suppose it isn't."

"I'd sooner it was yours than Eeyore's," said Piglet.

"So would I," said Pooh.

"H—hup!" said Roo again.

"AS—I—WAS—SAYING," said Eeyore loudly and sternly, "as I was saying when I was interrupted by various Loud Sounds, I feel that——"

"Here it is!" cried Christopher Robin excitedly. "Pass it down to silly old Pooh. It's for Pooh."

"For Pooh?" said Eeyore.

"Of course it is. The best bear in all the world."

"I might have known," said Eeyore. "After all, one can't complain. I have my friends. Somebody spoke to me only yesterday. And was it last week or the week before that Rabbit bumped into me and said 'Bother!' The Social Round. Always something going on."

Nobody was listening, for they were all saying "Open it, Pooh," "What is it, Pooh?" "I know what it is," "No, you don't" and other helpful remarks of this sort. And of course Pooh was opening it as quickly as ever he could, but without cutting the string, because you never know when a bit of string might be Useful. At last it was undone.

When Pooh saw what it was, he nearly fell down, he was so pleased. It was a Special Pencil Case. There were pencils in it marked "B" for Bear, and pencils marked "HB" for Helping Bear, and pencils marked "BB" for Brave Bear. There was a knife for sharpening the pencils, and india-rubber for rubbing out anything which you had spelt wrong, and a ruler for ruling lines for the words to walk on, and inches marked on the ruler in case you wanted to know how many inches anything was, and Blue Pencils and Red Pencils and Green Pencils for saying special things in blue and red and green. And all these lovely things were in little pockets of their own in a Special Case which shut with a click when you clicked it. And they were all for Pooh.

"Oh!" said Pooh.

"Oh, Pooh!" said everybody else except Eeyore.

"Thank-you," growled Pooh.

But Eeyore was saying to himself, "This writing business. Pencils and what-not. Over-rated, if you ask me. Silly stuff. Nothing in it."

Later on, when they had all said "Good-bye" and "Thank-you" to Christopher Robin, Pooh and

Piglet walked home thoughtfully together in the golden evening, and for a long time they were silent.

"When you wake up in the morning, Pooh," said Piglet at last, "what's the first thing you say to yourself?"

"What's for breakfast?" said Pooh. "What do *you* say, Piglet?"

"I say, I wonder what's going to happen exciting *to-day*?" said Piglet.

Pooh nodded thoughtfully.

"It's the same thing," he said.

"And what did happen?" asked Christopher Robin.

"When?"

"Next morning."

"I don't know."

"Could you think and tell me and Pooh some time?"

"If you wanted it very much."

"Pooh does," said Christopher Robin.

He gave a deep sigh, picked his bear up by the leg and walked off to the door, trailing Winnie-the-Pooh behind him. At the door he turned and said "Coming to see me have my bath?"

"I might," I said.

"Was Pooh's pencil case any better than mine?"

"It was just the same," I said.

He nodded and went out ... and in a moment I heard Winnie-the-Pooh—*bump, bump, bump*—going up the stairs behind him.

THE END

FOR MORE ANIMAL ADVENTURES
BE SURE TO CHECK OUT
"THE ADVENTURES OF DOCTOR DOLITTLE"

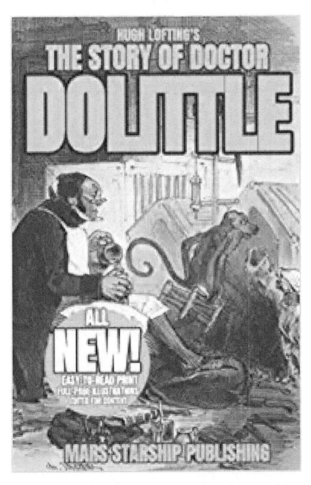

FOR MORE ANIMAL ADVENTURES
BE SURE TO CHECK OUT
"THE VOYAGES OF DOCTOR DOLITTLE"

www.MarsStarship.com

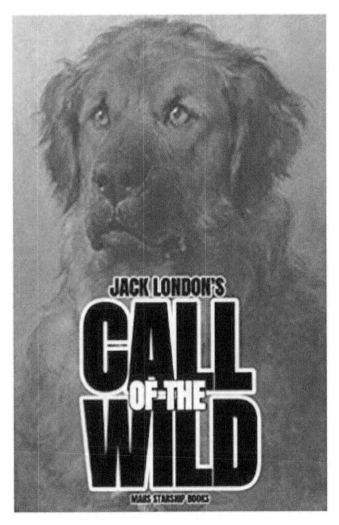

FOR MORE ADVENTURES FOR KIDS
BE SURE TO CHECK OUT
"ALICE IN WONDERLAND"

www.MarsStarship.com

Made in United States
North Haven, CT
04 October 2022